Grit is Good

A BOOK ABOUT PERSEVERANCE FOR KIDS

Written by Kristen Riddell
Illustrated by Deborah Faenza

First Edition

Text Copyright ©2021 Kristen Riddell
Illustrations Copyright ©2021 Deborah Faenza
Published by Kate Butler Books

www.katebutlerbooks.com

All rights reserved.

ISBN: 978-1-952725-67-8

No part of this book may be reproduced or transmitted in any form or by any means, electronic or mechanical, including photocopying, recording, or by any information storage and retrieval system—except by a reviewer who may quote brief quotations in a review to be printed in a magazine, newspaper or on the Web—without permission in writing from the publisher.

Design by Melissa Williams Design

For my sons, Charlie and Alex, who
have done, are doing, and can do hard things.

And to their best friend and sister,
Bailey the cockapoo puppy.

Find the candy corn hidden in each picture

My name is Charlie and I am 7 years old.

Today was the best day ever.

Crunch, crunch, crunch.

I found candy corn from Halloween in my pocket. It was delicious.

Pete let me be QB at recess and I even scored a touchdown.

My friends all cheered. Pride filled my chest like a balloon ready to burst!

Pop, pop, pop!

Most days at school Pete wants to be QB.

My head drops down, I feel my face getting as hot as a firecracker and then I shrug my shoulders and let him.

I really want to be a QB.

Pete throws as fast as a rocket.

He is the best football player in my class.

At recess, I run like whistling wind and try to catch the ball.

I stretch out my arms but sometimes I drop the ball. Pete's face crumples up and he looks like an angry elf.

He growls and tells me I can't catch anything.

It makes me want to catch even better.

It also makes me a little sad some days.

My Cockapoo puppy, Bailey, likes to lap my salty tears with her sandpaper tongue and that makes me giggle.

She is my very best friend.

Every night I ask my dad to practice football with me.

My dad is mammoth and indestructible. He hurls the best spirals. Night after night after night.

I ask my older brother, Will, to join us. Will is too busy playing video games.

He is 12 and likes to lie on his bed and eat hot Cheetos that are so peppery that they make my tongue sizzle.

Spicy!

I work so hard that my fingers feel like ice cubes. I practice, and practice, and practice until the sky is as black as my favorite crayon.

I know that if I keep practicing I will get even better at football. My mom told me that if you practice anything over and over you can eventually get good at it.

I cannot be stopped.

One day, Pete tackled me and pinned my shoulder to the ground and I felt the ball slipping from my sweaty fingers.

I didn't let Pete see the tears well up in my eyes. I looked at him and brushed the crispy leaves off my red polo uniform shirt.

"Good tackle, Pete," I said.

Pete looked at me with his eyebrows in a deep v shape. "Are you OK?" he questioned.

"Yep, I have grit. And Grit is good." I scooped up the ball and sprinted down the field.

When I become the best QB at school I will make sure to be as kind as Mother Theresa and not yell at my friends when the ball slips out of their fingers like slippery spaghetti.

I will even be a good friend and teach them how to catch it.

Maybe I will invite them to come over to practice with my mammoth dad.

I may even give them the next candy corn I find in my pocket.

Crunch, crunch!

Learning Connection

Tips for Parents and Educators

GRIT is the extra push that helps us to achieve our goals even after we experience failure. Along with resilience, **grit** is what helps us to try again after not reaching a goal.

Here are some tips to encourage grit in children:

- **Lead by example.** Share your struggles with trying new things and persevering. Let them hear about the stories from your youth when you had obstacles that you overcame.

- **Keep in mind that it is natural for children to feel discouraged at times.** Shielding children from frustration may not ultimately help them develop grit and perseverance. It is also important to let children know that failing is OK; some of life's biggest lessons are from not succeeding the first time.

- **Offer encouragement for effort and doing hard things.** Try saying, "You can do hard things" or, "I noticed your consistent effort with that project."

Seeing a child struggle can pull at your heartstrings, but this can help them learn to persevere. Making sure the challenge isn't too big and making sure to champion your child along the way is also important.

Made in the USA
Las Vegas, NV
24 June 2021